CLASS SiX
and the
EEL of
FORTUNE

Bloomsbury Education
An imprint of Bloomsbury Publishing Plc

50 Bedford Square
London
WC1B 3DP
UK

1385 Broadway
New York
NY 10018
USA

www.bloomsbury.com

BLOOMSBURY and the Diana logo are trademarks of Bloomsbury Publishing Plc

This paperback edition published in 2017

A catalogue record for this book is available from the British Library.

ISBN
PB: 978 1 4729 3941 8
ePub: 978 1 4729 3939 5
ePDF: 978 1 4729 3942 5

2 4 6 8 10 9 7 5 3 1

Typeset by Newgen Knowledge Works (P) Ltd., Chennai, India
Printed and bound by CPI Group (UK) Ltd, Croydon CR04YY

To find out more about our authors and books visit www.bloomsbury.com.
Here you will find extracts, author interviews, details of forthcoming
events and the option to sign up for our newsletters.

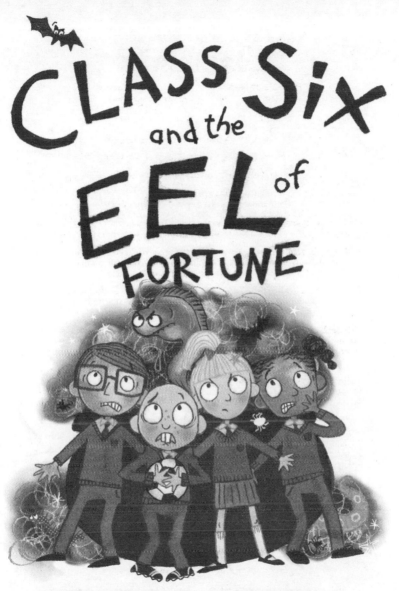

CLASS SIX
and the
EEL of
FORTUNE

SALLY PRUE
Illustrated by LORETTA SCHAUER

BLOOMSBURY EDUCATION
AN IMPRINT OF BLOOMSBURY
LONDON OXFORD NEW YORK NEW DELHI SYDNEY

Contents

Chapter One   7

Chapter Two   19

Chapter Three   27

Chapter Four   35

Chapter Five   41

Chapter Six   49

Chapter Seven   59

Chapter Eight   63

Chapter Nine   73

Chapter Ten   85

Chapter Eleven   89

Chapter Twelve   103

Chapter One

One Monday morning, a boy who looked like a
bald gerbil charged into the school playground.

'School!' he bellowed, punching the air.
'A whole new week! *Fantastic!*'

Two Class Three mums exchanged looks.

'He must come from ever such a bad home,'
one said.

'Oh no, Class Six are all like that,' said her
friend. 'Look at those girls.'

The girls had their heads busily together and
were saying things like *I'm going to have my magic
carpet pink, to match my bedroom.* Or *well, you're not
catching me kissing a frog, and that's final.* Or *I'm
going to ask to help with the unicorns at the school fair.*

Two more Class Six boys wandered into
the playground, one carrying a huge pork pie,

the other carrying a briefcase. The one with the briefcase was saying *oh no, it's impossible to get lost. Seven-League Boots all come with SatNav these days.*

'That's amazing,' said the first mum. 'Miss Broom must be such a good teacher. Still, all the teachers are good here, aren't they? I mean, I've never heard of Mr Wolfe or Mr Bloodsworth having any trouble with their classes, either.'

★　★　★

Miss Broom called Class Six's register, which was a waste of time because no one was ever absent.

'What are we going to learn today, Miss Broom?' asked Winsome, who was very studious and hard–working.

'Can we do some cooking for the school fair?' asked Slacker Punchkin.

Miss Broom hesitated, and Class Six suddenly noticed that her hair wasn't as bouncy as usual. Neither were her earrings or her smile. Not only that, but her eyes were somehow reflecting the sad sound of lost kittens.

'Are you all right, Miss Broom?' asked Anil, keen as always to get down to business.

The only answer was a sloshing washing-machine noise from the second row. But that was just Slacker eating his pie.

'I'm afraid something terrible has happened,' said Miss Broom.

A large purple moth floated down from the rafters and wiped Miss Broom's eyes tenderly with its wings.

Slacker Punchkin went pale.

'Nothing's gone wrong with the school dinners, has it?' he asked, hoarsely.

'Or Algernon?' asked Emily, who was always worried about everything. Algernon the snake was the Class Six pet.

'No, it's not the dinners,' said Miss Broom. 'And dear Algernon is very well, Emily. No, it's Mr Munsta. I'm afraid he's completely lost his head.'

Mr Munsta was Chairman of the School Governors.

'Really?' asked Jack, rather pleased, because Jack was himself known for doing silly things. 'What's he done?'

'Well, when he went to bed he left his head on the shelf, as usual, and somehow it must have fallen into the bin.'

'Oh, *poor* Mr Munsta!' said Emily.

'Well, it could have been worse,' said Miss Broom. 'It's turned up safe and sound at a recycling centre in China, but without his head Mr Munsta can't use his passport, so he's going to have to swim and walk all the way to get it.'

'But that'll take *months*,' said Anil.

'Yes,' said Miss Broom. 'So he's had to give up his job as Chairman of the School Governors.'

Class Six considered this. It was fun watching Mr Munsta scare away school inspectors, but other than that they didn't see him very often.

Jack shrugged.

'I suppose it'll be a bit boring having everyone in the school with just the one nose,' he said. 'But...'

'Will you really miss him, Miss Broom?' asked Emily, sympathetically.

'Oh, it's not that,' said Miss Broom. 'No, the trouble is that now we need a new Chairman of the School Governors – and Mrs Knowall has started campaigning to get the job!'

Class Six groaned. Mrs Knowall was a volunteer helper. She was bad-tempered and nosy and horrible, and she came to school every week to tell the children how bad they were at reading, or to shout at them because their knees were too knobbly.

'I'm going to get shouted at *all the time*,' sighed Jack.

Anil always wore long trousers, but even so his eyes had gone wide with horror.

'Mrs Knowall?' he exclaimed. 'But if she gets the job of Chairman of the School Governors, she'll be able to come to school every day, and she'll be able to go anywhere she likes. And she will want everything to be normal and boring. If she's around no one will be able to do any mer-mer-mer-*marble cake*!'

No one in Class Six could say the word *magic* because of a spell, but everyone knew what he meant.

'Oh no!' said Jack. 'What's the point of having a wer-wer-wer-*winkle* – I mean a *war dance* – I mean a wer-wer-wer-*weasel wearing winter underpants* – oh blow it! – a *you-know-what* as a teacher if she can't do mar-mar-mar-*marzipan*?'

No one in Class Six could say *witch*, either.

Miss Broom wrung her hands.

'And I was planning for us to have such fun!' she said tearfully. 'I was going to turn us all

12

into seagulls so we could swoop down and frighten television presenters... and I thought it would be nice if you could all play a musical instrument...'

'I'd love to be able to play the clarinet,' said Winsome.

'Or the triangle,' said Jack, wistfully.

'... but Mrs Knowall will be *everywhere*,' went on Miss Broom. 'It'll be bad enough while she's running her campaign: she'll be constantly visiting the school to find out all she can about us. But once she's installed as Chairman of the School Governors she'll be into absolutely everything. She'll leave no stone unturned. And you know what you can find under stones in *this* school.'

Class Six knew: luminous toads; very angry potatoes; even the occasional gnome.

Winsome took in a deep breath.

'Perhaps Mrs Knowall won't get the job,' she said, bravely.

'Oh, but she will,' Miss Broom said, distraught. 'She's always telling everybody how she's best friends with Mr Obadiah Ogersby, the District Chief Inspector of Schools. She's *bound* to get the job. And *I'm* bound to get the sack if Mrs Knowall notices anything magical going on!'

'So that really does mean...' began Slacker Punchkin, but it was too awful to say out loud.

Miss Broom nodded so violently that the spider holding back her hair nearly fell into her mug of coffee.

'Yes,' she said, almost in a wail. 'It means that from now on, *this is going to have to be a magic-free school!*'

* ★ ★ ★

Class Six were no longer sparkling with joy and enthusiasm when they went out for break. They had all the bounce and zip of damp zombies.

'No mer-mer-mer-*meerkat*s,' said Anil, heavily.

Rodney blinked round at his classmates. He was so slow that he was always a couple of conversations behind the others.

'But there have *never* been any meerkats,' he pointed out.

'I didn't mean *meerkats*, Rodney,' snapped Anil, irritated, 'I meant mer-mer-mer-*mushy peas!*'

'Mop heads!' said Slacker.

'Mangers!' said Winsome.

'Hairnets!' said Jack.

Everyone glared at him.

'Hairnets doesn't even begin with an *m*,' said Serise, crushingly.

Serise never had much patience with anyone, and Jack needed mountains of the stuff.

Jack glared back.

'I can't help it if I'm extra sensitive to mer-mer-mer-*merrily merrily merrily merrily, life is but a dream*! Oh drat!'

Winsome, who was very responsible, spoke to Rodney slowly and calmly.

'We're upset because Miss Broom won't be able to use her... her special powers... to make school such fun,' she explained. 'So no more flying.'

Rodney breathed through his mouth for a while.

'But people *can't* fly,' he pointed out.

Winsome stayed very calm.

'Not usually,' she agreed. 'But *we've* flown, haven't we? You remember. In the hall.'

'Oh,' said Rodney. 'In the hall.'

Everyone gave a sigh of relief. Getting anything into Rodney's head was hard work, and often impossible, but it looked as if Winsome had done it.

'Yes,' they all said. 'In the hall.'

Rodney gave a big fat grin.

'Oh, that was just an optical illumination,' he said.

Anil opened his mouth to say *do you think it was an optical illusion when Robin Hood came in and gave us that archery lesson?* But in the end he couldn't be bothered.

'How will we *survive* without mer–mer–mer–matchsticks?' Jack asked, hollowly.

They all shook their heads.

'Well, this means our trip to the moon's off,' said Slacker, through a bun. 'I was really looking forward to trying green cheese, too.'

'I did think the teachers were a bit quiet,' said Winsome, thoughtfully. 'Usually you can't stop Mr Wolfe chasing after balls, but today he slunk past Class Four's footie game with hardly a twitch of his ears.'

'Miss Elwig's songs were really sad this morning, too,' said Emily. Miss Elwig was the head teacher. She went around in a wheelchair with a blanket over her lower half, spent ages looking in her mirror, and always smelled strongly of fish.

'They're always sad,' pointed out Serise, irritably. 'They're all about dead sailors.'

'Yes,' said Anil, 'but she doesn't usually sound quite so much as if Mr Bloodsworth's just bitten her in the neck.'

Everyone sighed.

'What on earth are we going to *do*?' asked Slacker, blowing crumbs all over everybody.

But none of them had any answer to that.

Chapter Two

When Class Six got back to the classroom they found Miss Broom cutting up sheets of blotting paper.

'We're going to do a project about plants,' Miss Broom told them, apologetically.

Class Six considered this.

'Is there a plant that turns old ladies into beetles?' asked Jack.

Miss Broom looked gloriously happy for a moment – but then she looked glum again.

'Yes, there is,' she admitted. 'But we couldn't possibly...'

Anil tutted.

'Why are the *useful* things never *allowed*?' he demanded.

'Because they get found out,' said Miss Broom. 'Still, we *are* going to do something *quite* magical.'

'Really?' said Slacker. 'Like flying to Bouncy Beach to pick some Springy Strawberries to make some Jumping Jam for the school fair?'

'Not exactly.' Miss Broom smiled a brave smile. 'I found this old packet of seeds in the cupboard, so I thought we'd grow some runner beans.'

So Class Six put some blotting paper in jam jars, wedged a bean between the paper and the glass, and then watered the pots. It was quite interesting, but it wasn't *magic*.

'Now what?' asked Serise, when they'd arranged the jam jars on the windowsill.

'Now we wait until they begin to grow,' said Miss Broom.

Jack squatted down and peered closely at his bean.

'I don't think my bean likes water much,' he said. 'Shall I try it with some orange squash?'

'I'm afraid nothing is going to happen for at least a week, Jack,' explained Miss Broom.

'A *week*?' echoed Slacker Punchkin. 'But I'm hungry!'

'Good grief. How long do the *walker* beans take?' asked Serise.

'Can't you make it harvest time straight away?' asked Anil.

Miss Broom looked completely woebegone.

'I could,' she said, 'but I just don't dare. I can't risk it. I'm so sorry, my dears, but the wheel of fortune has turned against us. Just think, Mrs Knowall might be in the school on her campaign trail at this very minute. She might be right outside the door – and Mrs Knowall has ears like satellite dishes and a nose like a vacuum cleaner. Every hair on her chin is as sensitive as a bat's whisker. Her eyes are as sharp as ogres' tusks and her fingers are so skinny they can winkle the secrets out of people's mouths without them even noticing. The smallest sign of magic –'

– but before she could say any more, something behind the children began to rustle.

Class Six spun round. Most of the jam jars were still sitting on the windowsill being boring, but from one of the jars – the children's eyes opened as wide as fried eggs – a huge shoot was growing. As they watched, a tendril as thick as Algernon's waist curled upwards and took hold of one of the central-heating pipes.

Several people screamed, but they were all pleased, really. Magic, this was *magic*! They'd thought school was going to be dull and ordinary, but here was magic, lovely magic, after all.

Only Anil looked terrified and appalled.

'You know what this means, don't you?' he said, palely.

The shoot was growing so fast it had already reached the ceiling. The tip nosed its way this way and that for a moment, and then it drew back a little before punching its way cleanly right through the roof.

'That a mer-mer-mer I mean an *enchanted* bean somehow got in among the packet of ordinary ones?' asked Jack, brushing plaster dust out of his hair.

'Things did get in a muddle that time the cockroaches held their party in the magic cupboard,' Miss Broom admitted.

'Yes, but it's worse than that,' said Anil.

'You mean Mrs Knowall might catch us being... not ordinary?' asked Winsome.

'It's worse than *that*,' said Anil.

'Because we're going to be eating beans for school dinners every day until the summer holidays?' asked Slacker, as the bean plant burst into long streamers of scarlet flowers.

'Worse than that!' said Anil.

Jack blinked at him.

'I don't think there *is* anything worse than that,' he said. 'Have you been in the same room as Rodney when he's been eating beans?'

A long *boooom* sounded from somewhere above them and sent all the jam jars rattling.

'Thunder!' said Emily, who was frightened of everything.

'That did sound like thunder,' agreed Winsome, 'except... it's funny, but there seemed to be words in it, somehow.'

'Something about a fee,' said Rodney, surprising everybody by knowing what was going on.

'I knew it,' whispered Anil, who'd gone the colour of terrified toffee.

'A *fee*?' echoed Miss Broom, puzzled. 'Well, I'm sure I've paid my magic bill.'

The rumbling came again. It echoed so much it was hard to hear, but again, amazingly, it was Rodney who worked out what it was saying. One reason his brains didn't work very well was because his ears took up so much of his head space.

'It's saying *fee fie fo fum*,' Rodney said importantly.

There was a moment's complete silence, and then someone screamed *incoming giant!* and everyone started panicking. Jack began running round in circles shouting *an axe! Someone get an axe!* and Winsome and Anil fell over each other running for the scissors cupboard.

Serise dived under the nearest table.

'I hate to tell you this, but that's definitely a giant's bum,' she said, peering up through the hole in the roof.

Emily freaked.

'A giant!' she shrieked. 'A huge giant! It's coming, it's coming! It's going to eat us all up! Aaaarrrggghhhh!'

Her scream was drowned out by more thunder.

'*That* time it said *I smell the blood of an Englishman*,' reported Rodney, happily.

'What if you're not an Englishman?' asked Anil, desperately.

'But you are,' said Slacker.

'Yes,' agreed Anil, 'but –'

'Yeah, even your parents come from Watford,' said Jack. 'Like your grandparents.'

Slacker suddenly bellowed *weed killer!* and lunged for the door, but before he could get there a tendril as strong as a skipping rope looped itself neatly round his neck.

Slacker clutched helplessly at the tightening vine.

Through the hole in the roof the giant's enormous feet and ragged socks could now be seen quite clearly through the bright green leaves of the beanstalk.

'*Be he alive or be he dead –*' and then, with the whole class about to be strangled or eaten, things got even worse.

'*What's all this?*' demanded a scratchy voice from the doorway: and Class Six turned round to see an old lady wearing a brown suit and an expression like someone who's trodden in something nasty.

'Mrs Knowall!' gasped Winsome.

The whole class froze with horror.

There was a giant coming down to munch them all up – and now Miss Broom wouldn't be able to do any magic to stop it.

Chapter Three

Anil was the first to speak.

'Um... were you born in England, Mrs Knowall?' he asked, politely. 'Because if you were then perhaps you'd like to stand over there. So you can be... er... seen clearly.'

Mrs Knowall took no notice. She scowled round the room.

'What are all those untidy leaves doing blocking off the light?' she snapped. 'And why is there a hole in the ceiling?'

Everyone said the first thing that came to mind. Winsome blurted out something about rainforests, Jack mentioned harvest festival ('*It's the middle of summer, dimbo,*' muttered Serise) and Anil started jabbering about a grow-your-own-lunch business. Unfortunately all of them spoke at the same time, and Mrs Knowall ignored them anyway.

'What's that fat boy doing on the floor?' she demanded.

'Dying, I think,' whispered Slacker, who was the colour of a bruised grape. Winsome went over and started trying to unwind the tendril from his neck.

The bean plant rustled, an oddly menacing sound, just as if there were a giant climbing down it – and then an enormous boot came through the hole in the ceiling.

Emily screamed again, and everyone got as far away from the descending giant and Mrs Knowall as they could get.

Mrs Knowall put her hands on her hips.

'Chaos!' she said. '*Utter* chaos! Miss Broom, I shall be reporting this to my friend Mr Ogersby, the District Chief Inspector of Schools.'

'But... it's... it's educational!' said Anil.

'Global warming,' said Slacker, randomly. Well, it was the answer to pretty much every thing.

'Jack, could you pass me some scissors?' asked Winsome.

'Ooh yes, Slacker's eyes are beginning to go bulgy,' said Jack, with interest, handing over some from the scissors cupboard.

The rumbling sound came again, very close.

'Oh dear,' said Anil. 'Thunder. You'd better go... um... somewhere else, Mrs Knowall, before you get soaked.'

Another rumble.

'It's all right,' said Rodney, happily. 'I can understand it.'

'No you can't, Rodney. You're an idiot, remember?' said Serise, but he took no notice.

'It's saying: *Jack? Did someone just mention Jack? Oh, not that smelly little idiot again. I'm off!*'

'Hey,' said Jack. 'I'm a celebrity!'

Serise squinted up through the hole in the ceiling.

'The giant's climbing back up again,' she reported. 'Its bum only looks the size of a rhino's, now.'

'A *giant*?' yelped Mrs Knowall, her face scrunched up like a sneezed-on tissue.

'A giant *bean*,' said Miss Broom, swiftly. 'The class is... er... very keen on gymnastics, you see. That's why we've grown our own... climbing frame.'

Mrs Knowall stepped forward into the middle of the classroom.

'Do you suppose, Miss Broom, that I can't see that fat boy being strangled on the floor?' she asked, acidly. 'Really, I've never –'

And then it happened. There was a new surge of rustling, and the beanstalk began to sway backwards and forwards like a belly dancer in a high wind. Serise shaded her eyes.

'The giant's definitely climbing upwards,' she said. 'His nostrils only look as big as soup bowls now. And I think he's winding up the beanstalk as he goes.'

It was true: the tendrils of the beanstalk were unwinding themselves neatly from the pipes and rafters – and from Slacker's throat – and they were withdrawing through the hole in the roof.

'But how can the giant be pulling up a plant he's standing on?' asked Anil, blinking.

'Mer-mer-mer-mer-mer-mer –' said Jack. 'Mer-mer-mer-*mud baths*. Oh blow it. You know how.'

There was a *plop* as the beanstalk's root pulled itself out of its jam jar, and then, no one quite knew how, the root gave itself a flick and Mrs Knowall was suddenly flying backwards through the classroom doorway and right out into the corridor.

Slacker kicked the door shut as a series of loud bangs from overhead told Class Six that the giant was mending the roof.

Everyone stood up, took deep breaths, looked round... and saw to their amazement that everything was completely back to normal.

Well, Slacker was the size of an airship, but then he always had been.

'Phew!' said Rodney. 'That was lucky! I suppose that big man must have fallen out of a helicopter.'

Class Six stared at him in even more amazement than usual.

'*What?*' demanded Scrise. 'Then where do you think all those leaves came from?'

'He must have caught hold of a tree branch as he came down,' said Rodney. 'Then the branch bounced back and so off he went, zooming off up to the helicopter again.'

'Oh, good grief,' said Anil.

'At least we're safe,' said Winsome.

'Safe?' echoed Miss Broom. 'Oh, if only we were! What *ever* are we going to do about Mrs Knowall?'

Class Six looked at the closed door. There was no sound coming from the other side.

'What if she's dead?' asked Emily, unhappily.

Anil looked at Emily as if she were mad.

'What if she's *not*?' he said.

In the end Winsome tiptoed out to investigate. She found Mrs Knowall upside down in the spare PE-kit box.

She helped Mrs Knowall out and took her gently to the secretary's room. Miss Jeanie the school secretary was very calm and kind, even when Mrs Knowall started talking about giants and beanstalks.

'I think we'd better get you to A&E,' said Miss Jeanie. 'Knocks on the head can be nasty.'

Mrs Knowall batted Miss Jeanie's thermometer away.

'I know what I saw,' she said, scowling, 'and I tell you I shall be keeping a *very* sharp eye on Class Six and Miss Broom. Giants in the classroom? Beanstalks running amok? I give you warning, Miss Jeanie: by the time I've finished here *this will be a respectable school*!'

★   ★   ★

'Respectable?' said Anil, in horror, when Winsome told them all about it. 'But that means *boring*!'

The teachers shook their heads when they heard the news, and Miss Elwig started singing a very sad song about a winkle with bad breath.

'It's the school fair that's the worst problem,' said Mr Bloodsworth. 'We need every penny the fair can make to buy our... um... ingredients. But how can we hold an extra-special money-raising fair, with unicorn rides and magic cakes and sea-serpent rides, if Mrs Knowall's nosing around?'

'Oh, oh, why did this have to happen noooooooooooooowwww?!' asked Mr Wolfe.

Miss Elwig shook her head, causing a sea anemone in her hair to wave its tentacles crossly.

'I really can't see how the school is going to survive. Whatever can we *do*?' she groaned.

'Only one thing,' said Miss Jeanie, seriously. 'Some really clever magic to bamboozle even the nosiest of noses. Miss Broom: saving the school is down to you.'

Miss Broom nodded, but she thought about Mrs Knowall's beady eyes and super-sensitive nostrils, and she felt very worried indeed.

Chapter Four

Mrs Knowall was held in hospital for a few days (she kept saying odd things about giant beanstalks) and by the time she was allowed home Miss Jeanie had worked out a Mrs Knowall alarm system. Whenever the old busybody came stomping sourly down the drive Miss Jeanie or Miss Elwig, whose offices were by the entrance porch, would alert the classroom pets, who would make alarm calls (Algernon hissed his) and then everything interesting would stop at once and the children would start chanting spellings.

'B – U – S – Y – B – O – D – Y: **BUSYBODY!**' Class Six would chorus, while Mrs Knowall glared at them, full of suspicion and loathing.

Soon Class Six and Miss Broom even began to feel safe enough to do a little magic. Miss Broom was of course very busy with arrangements for the school fair, but she took Class Six down a meerkat burrow (which was very dark and surprisingly smelly, but the babies were cute). The children also designed an anti-bullying campaign aimed at goblins, and got their noses upgraded with Micro-Magic GPS, which meant it was impossible for them to get lost.

But then one terrible day everything went wrong.

It was hard to say whose fault it was ('*Just a turn of the wheel of fortune,*' said the headmistress Miss Elwig, sadly, afterwards, between verses of a sorrowful song about a prawn with no friends), but you could hardly blame Emily for having the screaming abdabs and throwing the key to the carpet store into the wildlife pond when a purple frog jumped on to her head from the middle of the magic carpet she was carrying across the playground (magic carpet lessons took place outside because of the danger of low ceilings).

Anyway, losing the keys didn't matter because Miss Elwig loved spending time underwater. Rodney pushed her across the playground in her wheelchair and she slithered into the green water as easily as a fish.

'Now, Rodney,' Serise said. 'Did you see Miss Elwig's tail, or are you a *complete* idiot?'

A slow smile spread across Rodney's face.

'A tail? That's silly,' he said. 'Those were flippers.'

'But there was only one of them!' squawked Anil. 'And it was all scaly! And it smelled of fish!'

'Yes. It's funny what people wear, isn't it,' said Rodney, happily. 'My Auntie Vera's got a string vest.'

Anyway, none of this would have mattered if the dragons' claw clippings had been delivered. Now why they were late, whether the claw-clippings delivery man had been eaten by a troll, or whether the dragons had been out fighting knights in armour when the claw-clippings man called, no one knew; but the fact was that the school was down to its last packet of claw clippings – and of course you can't turn yourself into a porcupine without *those*. So Miss Jeanie the school secretary, not knowing that Miss Elwig was at the bottom of the pond cooing over some sweet little tadpoles, nipped neatly into her brass lamp and went off to find some dragons.

This meant that no one knew Mrs Knowall was on the premises until she came face to face with the cave man. Class Six was having a history class by then, and Miss Broom had taken the classroom back in time so they could meet a Neanderthal man. He had just finished going through Health and Safety ('*Right then, you lot, a mammoth's trunk can't half give you a nasty swipe, so be sure to stand well back.*'), when there was a noise as if someone had trodden on a woolly rhinoceros's foot and a fierce-eyed creature appeared through the swirling snow and charged straight for them.

Everyone screamed and got out of its way, and it was only at the very last moment, with the Neanderthal about to throw his spear, that they realised the approaching creature wasn't a sabre-toothed tiger after all, but Mrs Knowall – and they only realised *that* when she screeched *this is an utter disgrace!*

It was perfectly clear who was to blame for saving Mrs Knowall from being speared by the Neanderthal: it was partly Winsome, who shouted *watch out!* at the top of her voice, and partly Miss Broom, who began shouting something beginning *abracadabra...*

... and in a moment the Neanderthal, and the snowy hillside they were all standing on,

had swirled itself round into a tornado that spun swiftly through the whiteboard and disappeared.

There was a moment of complete silence apart from the sound of Mrs Knowall going *tcha!*

'Ah, Mrs Knowall,' said Miss Broom, as brightly as she could. 'Um... you arrived just in time to see our... our new...'

'... virtual-reality program,' said Anil, cleverly.

'Yeah,' said Serise. 'It's, like, technology... stuff.'

'Computers,' said Jack.

'Coding,' said Winsome, earnestly.

Mrs Knowall did her *tcha!* thing again, and bent down creakily to pick something up off the floor.

She held it out triumphantly. It was steaming.

'Virtual?' she demanded. 'New technology? *New?* Because what *I'd* call this, Miss Broom, is a *very* real and *very* definite lump of mammoth poo!'

And it was, too.

Chapter Five

The next morning, when Class Six arrived for registration, they found Miss Elwig sitting in Miss Broom's place.

'I'm afraid Miss Broom won't be able to come to school for a while,' said Miss Elwig, very seriously.

Class Six gasped in dismay.

'But what about our trip to the end of the rainbow?' asked Serise. 'I was going to buy some hair clips with my share of the pot of gold!'

'And who's going to make Slacker see-through so we can watch what happens to his dinner after he's eaten it?' asked Jack.

Miss Elwig sang a few lines of a gloomy song about a pirate whose parrot had gone bald.

'I'm afraid we'll have to cancel those activities,' she said.

'But where's Miss Broom?' asked Winsome.

'At training college,' answered Miss Elwig, shaking her head regretfully. Three shrimps and a sardine fell out of her hair. She picked them up and ate them, absently.

'But Miss Broom is the best teacher we've ever had,' said Anil.

'*Easily* the best,' said Jack. 'I mean, even *Rodney* remembers to use the pointy end of his pencil now. Usually.'

'I know, I know,' said Miss Elwig. 'But the wheel of fortune has turned against us and the school is in terrible danger.'

'From Mrs Knowall?' whispered Emily.

'That's right. If Mrs Knowall sees one more thing that looks at all... unusual... then she'll tell her friend Mr Ogersby, and he's in charge of all the teachers in the area. He'd be bound to have me sacked, and Miss Broom as well. There'll be a new head teacher brought in, someone quite normal, and then you can be sure it won't be long before Mr Wolfe and Mr Bloodsworth and Miss Jeanie are dismissed, too.'

It was too awful to think about.

There was an odd gulping noise from Miss Broom's desk. Miss Elwig opened the drawer and lifted out a large snake with crosses all the way down his back. Miss Elwig stroked him comfortingly.

'There there, Algernon,' she said. 'We hope Miss Broom will be back soon.'

'But she *will* be back soon,' said Jack. 'Won't she?'

Miss Elwig hesitated.

'This has come at a terrible time,' she explained. 'The school fair is only four days away, and everyone comes to our fair —'

'Of course they do!' said Slacker. 'It's brilliant. The cakes... they're so light!'

'My brother Morris got blown right up into a tree last year after he scoffed three,' added Serise.

'I like the worm-charming,' said Jack. 'It's amazing. I'd never have thought worms could tap-dance.'

'Yes,' said Miss Elwig, 'it's very special, and that's why people come and spend so much money. But how can we be special if Mrs Knowall is around? And if the school fair is dull and ordinary, people won't spend nearly so much — and how will we afford all the barrels

of toad slime, the newt bogeys, and the tins of the burps of a tiger that has only ever eaten pork chops with mushroom ketchup, then?'

Slacker licked his lips.

'I like ketchup,' he said.

Miss Elwig sighed. 'If only Miss Broom could be at the fair she could cast Mrs Knowall into an enchanted sleep –'

'– and then I could throw rotten tomatoes at the old bat,' said Jack, with feeling.

'And I, Jack, would join you,' said Miss Elwig with another sigh. 'But what can we do? The stalls that make most of the money are run by the... less ordinary of us.'

'Like the flying ladies who sell the make-you-beautiful blusher,' said Serise.

'Like the green men who do the firework rides,' said Jack.

'Like the brownies who make the brownies,' said Slacker.

'Exactly,' said Miss Elwig. 'It's going to be bad enough not having Miss Broom to make the cakes and order the sea serpent. Those are two of the most important attractions, and our profits are going to be seriously down without them. But it will be hopeless without the other special stalls.'

Slacker squared his shoulders.

'Don't worry about the cakes, Miss Elwig,' he said. 'I've done lots of baking with Miss Broom. Class Six can organise the cake stall.'

'And why does it have to be Miss Broom who orders the sea serpent?' asked Anil, puzzled.

'Because none of the other teachers has a postal address,' Miss Elwig explained. 'My home is at the bottom of the reservoir, Mr Bloodsworth lives in the graveyard, and Mr Wolfe lives under a picnic bench in the middle of the woods. I'm afraid the credit card people don't like it at all.'

'Algernon looks after Miss Broom's credit card,' said Jack. 'I'm sure he'll let us borrow it, as it's a good cause.'

Anil began walking thoughtfully up and down.

'Class Six can make the cakes and order the sea serpent,' he said, 'and Class Six will also have to stop Mrs Knowall seeing things at the fair. You grown-ups won't be any good at it because you're all so... special... to start with.'

'Wonderful,' said Winsome, earnestly. 'But... different.'

'Weird,' said Jack.

'Gross,' suggested Serise.

'In a good way,' said Slacker Punchkin.

'But the thing is, *we're* all quite normal,' went on Anil.

'Normal?' said Serise, raising an eyebrow. 'Rodney?'

'Well, at least he doesn't keep turning into a wolf, or getting urges to bite people in the neck!'

'But how on earth can we stop Mrs Knowall from noticing that the person holding up the helter-skelter is a giant?' asked Jack.

Miss Elwig opened her mouth to start another sad song, probably about a shark with toothache, but Anil didn't give her a chance.

'We'll tell Mrs Knowall that the person holding up the helter-skelter is a pyramid of parents from the PTA *dressed up* as a giant,' he said.

They all stared at him.

'My dear Anil!' exclaimed Miss Elwig. 'I didn't know you were so devious. Or so cunning. Or dishonest. My dear boy, you're an absolute genius!'

And she suddenly burst into a little chorus about Myrtle the purple turtle.

It was actually quite jolly, for one of Miss Elwig's songs.

Chapter Six

There was a supply teacher sitting in Miss Broom's chair when Class Six got back to the classroom after break. He was a small, whiskery man with huge eyes, a tiny nose, a mustard waistcoat, and oddly baggy trousers.

He blinked round at the class.

'I understand you have a school fair to arrange,' he said, yawning.

'Um. Yes,' said Winsome, politely.

'Good. I'll leave you to get on with it, then,' he said, as he wriggled his large bottom into a more comfortable position on the chair and closed his eyes.

Nothing happened for a couple of minutes.

'So... aren't we going to have any lessons?' asked Jack, at last.

The man started, and opened an eye.

'Lessons? Ah, yes, I should have said. I understand you've been having trouble with some dreadful woman... a Mrs Knowall, is that right? So you must tell me if she should happen to come along. I have several *extremely* dull lessons up my sleeve that should satisfy even the nastiest school governor. Just push the third button on my waistcoat and I shall spring to life.'

'Spring to *life*?' echoed Emily, paling.

The man smiled. 'Oh, I'm not a ghost or anything like that. No, I'm Mr Hazel, and I'm largely dormouse. It makes me really *very* cheap to hire.'

Class Six looked at each other.

'Well, goodnight, then,' said Mr Hazel, and settled himself down once more.

Mr Hazel did say just one more thing before he started snoring. It was *do wake me up at home time, won't you.*

★ ★ ★

'Well, that *wheel of fortune* thing people keep going on about has finally rolled our way,' said Jack, with satisfaction. 'This means we can spend the whole day playing football!'

'No, Jack,' said Anil, firmly. 'This means we can spend the whole day saving the school.'

'But... but... but *we're only little!*' said Emily, her bottom lip quivering.

Anil marched up and down importantly.

'We must make a list,' he said. 'Most of the attractions at the fair are run by outside people, like the feed-the-troll bins and the unicorn rides –'

Winsome made a note: *refreshments for unicorns?*

'– but anything that's usually arranged by Miss Broom we have to organise ourselves.'

'Well, I'll start work on the cake stall,' said Slacker Punchkin, licking his lips.

'Can you make Toasted Lean Tarts, like Miss Broom does?' asked Serise. 'You know, the ones that make you thinner?'

'Yes, we need Toasted Lean Tarts, they sell like hot cakes,' said Jack. 'They must make tons of money.'

Slacker Punchkin turned to the cupboard where Miss Broom kept her cauldron, his mouth set in a determined line.

'Well, I can jolly well try,' he said.

Most of the teachers did quite ordinary things at the fair, like running the raffle or judging the fancy dress (the school fair had *easily* the best fancy-dress parade in town, with fairies who really seemed to be flying, and dragons who could toast marshmallows as they walked along). Mr Wolfe and Mr Bloodsworth ran the sea-serpent ride, but Miss Broom, as Miss Elwig had told them, ordered the sea serpent.

'I like the sea-serpent ride,' said Rodney. 'I like seeing the old toilets in Atlantis. And the barnacles.'

'Ah, right,' said Serise. 'You saw Atlantis. From a sea serpent. *Now* tell me you don't believe in mer-mer-mer-*mumps*.'

'Of course I don't,' said Rodney. He put the blunt end of a pencil into his ear and began to turn it round and round as if he was sharpening it. He often did things like that. 'That was just a bicycle confusion.'

'A *bicycle*... oh, never mind,' said Anil. 'Let's see what Slacker can do with the Lean Tarts, shall we?'

★ ★ ★

The difficult bit about making Lean Tarts was picking the thistles. Well, that and persuading the moths to show you where they'd left their cast-off cocoons. Even so, it wasn't long before the classroom was filled with the delicious scent of crisping cobwebs.

'Here we are,' said Slacker, at last, taking a baking tray out of the cauldron. 'They just need a swirl of bats'-blood icing now.'

'Oh, poor little bats!' said Emily, welling up.

'Oh no, it's all right, it comes from cricket bats,' explained Slacker. 'They don't feel a thing.' And soon the pile of tarts was gleaming with scarlet frosting.

'Can I have one?' asked Jack, licking his lips.

'No you can't, they're for the fair,' said Anil, severely. 'We need every penny we can raise. Our education's at stake!'

'We won't get much education if we're in jail for poisoning people,' pointed out Scrise. 'Those tarts have got a lot of scorpion poo in them, don't forget.'

Winsome nodded.

'We must be responsible,' she said. 'We can't risk hurting members of the public.'

Anil tutted.

'Oh, all right, then. Jack!'

'What?'

'You can eat one.'

Class Six watched as Jack picked up a glistening tart and took a huge bite.

'What's it like?' asked Slacker, with professional interest.

Jack's answer came through a cloud of crumbs and spiders' hairs.

'Fantastic!' he said. 'It tastes of candyfloss and maple syrup and strawberries... and, hang on, there's a bit of chocolate in there, too. And cake. Lots of buttery cake with a toffee aftertaste, and...'

The first sign that something wasn't quite right was the change in Jack's face. It was largely hidden behind his Lean Tart, but...

'His nose is getting flatter,' whispered Emily to Winsome.

Jack was too busy rabbiting on about golden syrup and liquorice allsorts to take any notice, but soon other odd things began happening.

'I don't think his eyes are quite as bulgy as usual,' said Serise.

'And look at his knees,' said Anil. 'They're usually like doorknobs, but now they look almost... *normal*.'

Winsome moved round so she could see Jack sideways and gave a gasp.

'He's getting thinner!' she said.

'Oh, that's good,' said Slacker Punchkin. 'I was afraid they wouldn't work. Now I come to think about it, I'm pretty sure I used the wrong type of toadstool.'

'No,' said Serise, who'd joined Winsome. 'He's not getting thinner like that. Jack, turn sideways. See? He's getting *thinner!*'

And then they all saw what she meant. Jack was the same height as before, but sideways on he was only a few centimetres thick. As they watched, he shrunk to the width of a paperback, and then a comic, and then a sheet of cardboard.

Anil hastily snatched the remains of the Lean Tart away from Jack before he vanished altogether.

Winsome was just saying *we'll have to make him sick*, when they heard bad-tempered heels clacking along the corridor.

'Mrs Knowall!' squeaked Emily.

Everyone moved at once. Anil shoved Jack against the wall and hissed *look like a painting!* Slacker slammed the magic-cupboard door shut on the cauldron, Winsome raced over to push the third button on Mr Hazel's waistcoat, and everyone else flung themselves into their seats.

When Mrs Knowall appeared in the classroom doorway it was to find Mr Hazel standing up and saying, in the most boring voice ever: 'Children must eat raw vegetables at least twenty-three times a day. Repeat after me: carrots, thirty calories per hundred grams; broccoli, thirty calories per hundred grams; cabbage, twenty-five calories per hundred grams...'

Mrs Knowall looked at the faces of the children, haggard with worry and shock, and smiled a little self-satisfied smile. Then she nodded politely to Mr Hazel, said something about being glad the children were learning something useful, and backed out.

'Phew!' said Slacker, once the door has closed behind her. 'That was close! But what on earth do we do now?'

Mr Hazel blinked round blearily.

'Oh, I'm sure you'll work something out,' he said. Then he sat down again, settled himself comfortably in his chair, and went back to sleep.

Chapter Seven

'*Work something out?*' said Serise. 'It's home time in fifteen minutes, and Jack's about the thickness of a cheese and onion crisp!'

Slacker squinted thoughtfully at Jack.

'Perhaps no one will notice,' he said.

'You must be joking,' said Jack. 'I'm going to my gran's tonight!'

'Well, just sit her down in front of a TV programme about celebrity illnesses,' said Anil. 'Old people don't notice anything if the telly's on.'

'*Gran* does,' said Jack, firmly. 'Anyway, she always wants to try out her judo moves on me, and I'm as thin as a sheet of loo roll! She'll tear me limb from limb!'

Outside a lorry with *Zoom-Zoom Balloons* written on the side was backing carefully into the car park.

'Balloons for the fair,' said Rodney, happily. 'I like balloons. Last year one took me up so high I could see all the way from the football ground to the zoo.'

'Zoo?' said Serise, distracted. 'What zoo?'

'I don't know. It had lions and zebras. And all the grass was yellow.'

Anil put his head in his hands.

'That was *Africa*, Rodney,' he said. 'The balloon took you up so high you could see *Africa*.'

'Oh no,' said Rodney. 'Africa's just somewhere in stories. Those giraffes and things must have been optional confusions.'

'The balloon man must have filled your *head* with gas, as well as the balloons,' muttered Serise.

Anil clicked his fingers.

'That's it!' he said. '*That's* the way to make Jack fatter! Wait here, you lot!'

And he ran out of the classroom.

★ ★ ★

It all worked remarkably well. Until –

'All right,' said Winsome. 'I think you're blown-up enough now, Jack.'

Jack took the balloon away from his mouth. Winsome hadn't let him suck the gas straight from the metal canister.

'He's still really skinny,' commented Serise, 'But at least his trousers are staying up.'

'All right,' said Winsome, 'take out the drawing pins, Anil.'

They'd pinned Jack's shirt to a display board to stop him from being blown over every time someone sneezed.

Anil prised out the pins.

'There we are,' he said. 'All done. I –'

'Eek!' Jack squawked.

'Oh no!' said everyone.

'Help!' Jack said, his head bumping against the ceiling and his feet dangling. 'I can't get down!'

'We should have known the gas would turn him into a balloon,' said Slacker.

'Emily!' said Winsome. 'You know the cupboard where Mr Bloodsworth keeps his long black cloak? Go and get it!'

'I'm not going to pretend to be a bat, not for anyone,' protested Jack. 'You must be joking! I might get eaten by an owl! Help! I want to come down!'

'And Rodney,' went on Winsome, 'you know those big pebbles by the pond? Get twelve of those, will you?'

'I'm not eating pebbles, either!' squawked Jack.

Luckily Mr Bloodsworth's cloak had deep pockets. Six pebbles in each pocket were just heavy enough to weigh Jack down so his toes touched the ground.

'But he's still very light,' said Winsome, wrinkling her forehead. 'Someone had better hold his hand on the way home in case he blows away.'

It caused a lot of argument, but in the end Emily, who was very soft-hearted, agreed to hold Jack's hand.

'Phew!' said Anil, as the bell rang for the end of the school. 'What a day! I hope tomorrow isn't like this.'

It wasn't.

The next day two people got eaten by a sea serpent.

Chapter Eight

Jack arrived at school the next morning still wearing Mr Bloodsworth's cloak.

'How are you?' asked Winsome, anxiously.

'Terrible,' said Jack. 'I nearly took off when I turned that windy corner by the shops. I could have ended up in Outer Mongolia. *And* I keep on burping.'

'You what?' said Winsome, in horror. 'Oh no!' She turned him round so she could see him sideways. 'He's getting thinner again!' she exclaimed. 'The gas must be leaking out!'

'I know it is,' said Jack, miserably. 'My trousers fell down twice just going down to breakfast.'

'What can we *do*?' said Emily.

Class Six looked at each other in despair – except for Rodney, who laughed.

'Everyone knows how to make themselves fatter,' he said. 'You just have to eat lots of sweets.'

Everyone took in a deep breath to say *but...* and then stopped.

'It has to be worth a try,' muttered Anil. He plucked a Toothrot bar from Slacker's vast fist. 'Here, eat that,' he said to Jack.

'Oi!' protested Slacker, but Jack had already taken his first bite. He burped five times while he was eating it, but by the end he might have been a little steadier on his feet.

'How much food have you got, Slacker?' asked Anil.

Slacker took some chasing, but Serise and Winsome were both fast runners and they managed to corner him. Slacker's rucksack contained a whole box of doughnuts and five pasties. Once Jack had eaten those he was heavy enough not to fall over, even when he got bashed by a passing butterfly.

'You'd better keep that cloak on until lunch time,' advised Winsome, 'and then we'll give you our puddings. I think you should be all right after that.'

★   ★   ★

Slacker fired up the cauldron as soon as Mr Hazel had called the register, then most of the class went out to collect ingredients for more cakes. Some people combed the field for worm casts, and some tried to persuade ladybirds to make footprints in a saucer of mud.

'Now we'd better book the sea serpent,' said Anil. So Winsome asked Algernon very politely if they could borrow Miss Broom's credit card, and Emily went to get Miss Jeanie's address book.

Anil flicked through the pages.

'*Salamanders, sandmen...* ah, here we are: *sea monsters*. There's a website.'

Anil sat down at one of the computers.

'Couldn't we have guinea-pig petting instead?' asked Emily, but Anil took no notice.

'There we are!' he said. 'It should be here after lunch.'

He sat back with a satisfied sigh.

'Arranging a fair is actually quite simple, isn't it,' he said.

Serise gave him a scornful look.

'Anil, you've just ordered a sea serpent,' she said. 'If anything is simple, it's *you*.'

★ ★ ★

65

There was a small plastic envelope on Mr Hazel's desk when they came in from lunch.

'*That* can't be the sea serpent!' said Slacker, picking it up.

Anil snatched the envelope and tore it open. A length of coloured tissue paper fell out and swooped gently down on to the desk.

'It's just a *picture*,' said Jack, very disappointed.

'Trust you to buy something from a dodgy site,' muttered Serise.

Winsome looked in the envelope and found an instruction sheet.

'*Just add a drop of water to bring the sea serpent to exciting life*,' she read.

Slacker was chomping on a Lean Tart. This latest batch seemed to be working well.

'We'll have to be really careful to keep it dry, then,' he said, spraying flakes of pastry everywhere. 'Just think: one single drop of water –'

A flake of pastry swerved elegantly up one of Rodney's nostrils. Rodney's shoulders twitched.

'No!' shouted Anil. 'Don't! Rodney, whatever you do, don't –'

Rodney sneezed, but the sound was drowned out by a long loud *pffffffft!* like a braking steam engine. Suddenly the room was full of a smell like mouldy football boots and they saw a dark waving shadow, which quickly proved to be cast by an enormous green sea serpent with metre-long fangs.

Rodney was the only person who didn't panic.

'Run!' shouted Jack.

'Run!' shouted everyone else.

Rodney smiled foolishly.

'Oh, don't worry,' he said. 'That's just a nautical pollution.'

It was the last thing he said before the serpent ate him.

★ ★ ★

The sea serpent kept striking out at people. It had just swallowed Jack's chair.

'Trust you to go and order a ferocious monster,' said Serise to Anil, meeting him under a table.

'It wasn't my fault!'

'Oh, well, that's all right, then,' snapped Serise. 'So are you just going to sit there while that thing eats us all?'

She crawled under a row of tables until she got to the front of the room, then reached out and pressed the third button of Mr Hazel's waistcoat.

'Oof!' said a mild voice.

'Mr Hazel!' said Serise. 'A sea serpent's just eaten Rodney!'

'Really?' said Mr Hazel, sleepily. 'A sea serpent? Mmm, yes. Magnificent beast!'

'*Magnificent?* It stinks of drains and old kippers!'

Mr Hazel yawned, slowly. 'Ah, yes, so it does. Um. Do you think you could get me a cup of coffee?'

'A sea serpent's eating people and you want *coffee?*' said Serise, in disbelief, but she crawled over to the magic cupboard.

Luckily the cauldron was still hot. Serise scooped out a cup of brown stuff (it *looked* like coffee and quite frankly she was past caring). Halfway back to Mr Hazel someone shouted *Anil, it's behind* – and then there was a blood-curdling scream.

'Ah, good, it's steaming nicely,' said Mr Hazel. 'Perfect. Now, just throw it over the sea serpent, will you?'

'Oh, yeah, right,' said Serise, scowling. 'What else do you want me to do? Make myself a paper hat with EAT ME on it?'

'I wouldn't waste any time,' advised Mr Hazel. 'He's just eaten another of your friends.'

Serise gave him a glare, but she hurled the cup of hot liquid over the nearest bit of the sea serpent.

There was a huge spurt of steam that blinded everyone, and then a giant cough – and then another – and then, quite suddenly, the air went completely clear.

The classroom went clear, too: instead of a huge, furious, stinking sea serpent there was just a lot of tumbled furniture and frightened children.

Two of the children were dripping wet and smelling of rotten fish and cabbage.

'It's Rodney and Anil!' shouted Jack. 'They're alive!'

Serise stepped back.

'They smell of serpent sick,' she said.

'It's worse than that,' said Slacker, backing away, too. 'They *are* serpent sick!'

Winsome picked up a long piece of tissue from the floor.

'The sea serpent's turned back into paper again,' she said, in amazement.

'Of course,' said Mr Hazel. 'Well, you know what happens if you put things in too-hot water, don't you.'

'You shrunk it,' said Slacker, admiringly. 'Brilliant!'

Winsome folded the sea serpent back into its plastic envelope and she'd just sealed it with seven layers of tape when sharp heels came clacking along the corridor.

Class Six stared round in horror. Anil and Rodney stunk of serpent sick, there were overturned chairs everywhere, and the magic-cupboard door was wide open.

Before they could move, a sharp nose appeared round the classroom door.

Then it recoiled.

'What's that disgusting smell?' demanded Mrs Knowall.

Mr Hazel went to the door.

'It's the dear sweaty children,' he told her. 'They've been taking some exercise.'

A hand came up to hold the nose.

'Um. Excellent,' said the voice, rather honkily. 'Good. Um... I'll leave you to it, then.' And the footsteps went away again.

'Phew. I thought I was dead, that time,' said Anil, weakly.

'We nearly *all* were,' said Winsome.

'Ah well,' said Mr Hazel, yawning. 'It turned out all right in the end. It's just one more turn of the wheel of fortune, my dears.'

Serise snorted.

'Yeah, right,' she said. 'And I wish someone could put a brake on the thing, because it's making me dizzy!'

Chapter Nine

Class Six spent the next two days busily baking cakes (the More-on-Top Cakes took *ages* because they were made with cast-off hairs from caterpillars who lived in oak trees) but at last it was the weekend and the day of the school fair dawned.

Class Six arrived bright and early – well, Rodney was just early. Anil stood by the school gates and directed all the stallholders as they arrived in vans or horseboxes, by broomstick or by carpet, to their places on the field.

'Slacker will show you the Treasure Hunt pitch,' Anil told a big bearded man with a wooden leg and a parrot.

'My sister loves the Treasure Hunt,' Slacker said, as he led the way across the grass. 'Well, she doesn't actually do much hunting, but she likes going to the tropical island. She's bringing some extra-strong sun cream specially.'

'A-harrrr!' said the bearded man.

'Fifty pee a go! Fifty pee a go!' said the parrot.

The unicorn rides were behind the wildlife garden.

'Could I help with the saddling?' asked Emily, shyly.

'If you like,' said a unicorn. 'And look, could you give my horn a bit of a polish while you're at it? It's covered in dust from that dirty old horsebox.'

Soon the Unlucky Dip (gifts guaranteed from a troll's dustbin), Trifle Range (splat the teacher!), Wing Boats, Balloon Flights, Worm Charming, Guess the Name of the Ugly Bad-Tempered Dwarf, Hook the Spook, Thirty-Eight-Point-Eight-Nine-Two Kilometre Boot Tours (yes, said the man running this stall, they were the same as Seven-League Boot Tours but he'd had to go metric because of the regulations) were all ready to go. Slacker Punchkin's cake stall was piled high with Toasted Lean Tarts, Curl Cakes, Pretty-Nose Pastries, More-on-Top Cakes, Bouncer Buns and Champion Cookies. The wellie-wanging pitch was marked out, the tea tent was up, and the tombola stall was piled high with dusty bottles of perfume and old tins of prunes – but that was because the tombola stuff was always donated by people's grannies.

The last stallholder to arrive was an old lady dressed in seaweed. She was carrying a goldfish bowl containing something long and brown.

Anil looked at his clipboard. There was only one stall not ticked off.

'Are you the fortune teller?' he asked.

The old lady's hair seemed to be made of seaweed, too.

'Oh no, dearie,' she said. 'No, my old brain can hardly keep track of the past, these days. No, it's Barry you want for that.'

Anil suddenly got the feeling that this was going to be a long day.

'Barry,' said the old lady, fondly, holding out the goldfish bowl. 'He's a marvel, is Barry. Look at the slime on him. Look at those teeny eyes. Yes, it's Barry who's the talent.'

'Um... right, er, Mrs... er...'

The old lady gave a sudden cackle of joy.

'I am Miss C Weed,' she announced, proudly, 'and this is Barry, the marvellous, the magnificent, the one and only *eel of fortune*!'

★   ★   ★

Anil escorted Miss C Weed to her place on the field. On the way back he met Winsome. She was carrying a sealed envelope as if she was expecting it to explode at any moment.

'It's the sea serpent,' she told Anil. 'Have you seen Mr Wolfe and Mr Bloodsworth?'

'I think they're marking out the squares for the Worm Charming,' said Anil. 'They're over there with that bunch of the stall–holders' friends.'

Winsome found Mr Bloodsworth and Mr Wolfe surrounded by a small crowd of... well, *people* wasn't exactly the right word. Some of them were ten feet taller than people, some of them had more tusks, and some of them had more warts and were wearing pointier hats. They were all watching intently as Mr Wolfe marked out squares of grass using string and wooden tent pegs.

Mr Bloodsworth seemed rather glad to get away from the wooden tent pegs. He took charge of the sea serpent and led the way to the pond where Miss Elwig was waiting.

'The sea serpent ate Anil and Rodney the other day,' Winsome told him, doubtfully.

'Ah, yes,' said Mr Bloodsworth, 'but then she was bound to be a bit bad-tempered if she had no sea to swim about in.'

Winsome looked at the school pond. It was two metres across and less than a metre deep.

Miss Elwig leaned over to whisper.

'I'm sure the sea serpent will find her way down into the sea, somehow.' And as she said this, an octopus's head popped out of the pond, waved an arm, winked and submerged again, slyly pulling a garden gnome with it as it went.

The gnome's friends thought that was *hilarious*.

'Right,' said Miss Elwig. 'Next. Rodney, dearest!'

Rodney was soon staggering backwards and forwards carrying stones from the rockery to the place where Mr Wolfe was setting up some speakers. Class Six had suggested booking a rock band to add a bit of atmosphere, and Miss Elwig seemed to think a rock band couldn't play without... rocks.

In another part of the field, Emily came across a large bundle of cloth hopping about and shouting rude things.

'I didn't know you were entering the fancy dress as a camel,' she said, putting down the unicorns' lemonade bucket, as Serise's head appeared out of a slit in the fabric.

'Camel?' spat Serise. '*Camel?* This isn't a camel costume, this is the fortune-telling tent!'

It turned out that Serise had got the tent upside down, inside out *and* back to front. By the time Emily had sorted it out there was only an hour to go until the start of the fair.

'It *should* be all right,' said Winsome, looking round at the bright grass and the cloudless sky. 'It's a pity about all those indigestion tablets and knee bandages on the tombola. Still, I suppose the zombies will like them.'

'The unicorns are lovely,' said Emily, happily. 'They're a bit fussy about their apples being the right shade of pink, but they're ever so friendly. I wish Miss Broom was here, though. For emergencies.'

Winsome sighed.

'I know. All those giants. They do look quite *nice* giants, but...'

'And I'm sure the trolls have only brought their hammers in case they want to hammer something,' said Emily. 'Something like... a nail. But not one on someone's finger. Obviously.'

'The ones that worry *me* are those tall pale people with the fangs and the long black coats,' said Serise, coming up.

'Them?' said Rodney, cheerfully, staggering past with another rock. 'That's just Mr Bloodsworth's family.'

'That's what I was afraid of,' said Serise.

But as it happened it wasn't the Bloodsworth family, or the trolls, or the giants, or even the sea serpent, that nearly gave them all heart attacks.

It was the band.

★ ★ ★

They were called *The Sirens*. They wore feathery, tight-fitting costumes (at least, they might have been costumes) and one had a turtle-shell harp, one had some sea-urchin bongos, one had a shell trumpet, and another had a xylophone made, apparently, out of whale bones.

'*They* aren't going to liven things up much,' Serise complained.

Slacker sighed.

'I wanted Miss Elwig to book some wizard guitarists,' he said, 'but she *would* have this lot. Huh! Just because they came with some silly guarantee about bringing in the crowds.'

'I hope they don't spend the whole afternoon wailing about drowned sailors, like Miss Elwig,' said Serise, gloomily. 'It would clear the field in five minutes.'

'Maybe they'll sing something cheerful,' suggested Slacker. 'Like sea shanties.'

'That would clear the field in *four* minutes,' said Serise.

The Sirens ate a hasty packed lunch ('I didn't know you *could* eat live lobsters,' said Jack, fascinated) and at ten minutes to opening time everything was set to go. Everyone was tremendously excited: even the sea serpent rippled with pleasure as Mr Wolfe and Mr Bloodsworth strapped on its twenty-seater saddle.

'Do you think the fair will go well?' Emily asked Miss C Weed.

'That'll be fifty pee, dear,' said Miss Weed.

Emily hesitated, then handed over the money.

Miss C Weed put her head close to Barry's goldfish bowl and seemed to be listening.

'Well, the next few minutes are going to be terrifying,' she said, as she tore two seaweedy strips off her dress and stuck them in her ears. 'What?' she demanded, taking one of them out again for a moment. 'What did you say, dearie?'

'I said, what about the next few minutes after that?' whispered Emily, palely.

'Oh, I can't tell you *that*,' said Miss C Weed. 'What do you expect for fifty pee?'

Across the field, *The Sirens* were tuning up. The harp was twanging like a broken bicycle wheel, and the shell trumpet sounded like a constipated elephant.

'What do you think?' Anil asked Slacker Punchkin.

'I think it's going to put everyone off their cake,' said Slacker.

At last the harpist opened her mouth at least four centimetres wider than any mouth should go, and began to sing. Well, it wasn't exactly singing: the sound was more like someone spin-drying a gibbon.

Everyone clapped their hands over their ears at once, but that didn't help because somehow the sound still found its way into their earholes.

It was sort of... itchy.

'It's like having ants in my ears,' said Jack, squirming.

'Hermit crabs,' winced Slacker, sticking iced buns on to the sides of his head.

'It's as if something's pulling me,' said Anil. 'Harder and harder...'

'I know,' said Serise. 'She sounds like a train whistle filled with gravy, but I just *can't stand still.*'

Winsome sat down on the grass, but within seconds she found herself crawling towards

The Sirens' rocky stage. 'I've just *got* to get closer,' she panted. 'I've *got* to!'

Now everyone on the field except for the sea serpent (which had no ears) and Miss C Weed was being pulled towards the band.

'I saw a film a bit like this once,' muttered Serise.

'How did it end?' asked Anil.

'How do you think? With the credits.'

'Of course!' exclaimed Winsome, as her arms and legs took her towards the stage. 'They're *sirens*! You know, like in that old Greek story. They lure people on to the rocks and then eat them!'

'I'm not going any closer,' said Anil, turning away – but his feet kept on going by themselves until he'd done a complete circle and was travelling in the same direction as before.

'Look!' gasped Jack.

There was something like an enormous jellyfish just outside the school gates.

'What is it?' whispered Emily.

Slacker shaded his eyes against the sun. Then he whistled.

'It's a *crowd*,' he said.

And it was: it was hundreds and hundreds of people walking down the road towards the sound of *The Sirens*' music. Thousands of people were handing over entrance money so they could come closer to *The Sirens*' song.

Class Six were at the edge of *The Sirens*' rocks, now.

'I don't want to be eaten,' gasped Emily – and at that moment, quite suddenly, the terrible twanging and wailing stopped.

The siren with the trumpet grinned down at them.

'How about that?' she asked. 'Works every time, yeah?'

She jerked her head at the vast crowd pouring through the gates.

'You can have jazz bands or brass bands,' she said, happily. 'You can even have elastic bands. But there's nothing, simply nothing, like *The Sirens* to bring in the crowds!'

And then she put her shell trumpet back to her lips and led the rest of the band into an afternoon of amazing feet-jiggling, talent-contest-winning rock music.

And they were absolutely brilliant.

Chapter Ten

The huge crowd, released from *The Sirens'* spell, streamed across the playing field. Some of the people were wearing sun hats, and some were carrying ladders, stethoscopes or cricket bats, because until they'd heard *The Sirens'* call they'd planned to spend their afternoon doing something entirely different.

Winsome waited by the school gates and watched out for Mrs Knowall's sour face. Winsome's job was to go round the fair with Mrs Knowall and make sure she didn't see anything unusual. The trouble was almost everything at the fair (apart from the knitted tea cosies and tins of metal polish on the tombola stall) *was* unusual.

The first things they saw after Mrs Knowall had arrived, appearing in the crowd like a

Brussels sprout in a bouquet of roses, were a couple of giants strolling over to the Trifle Range.

'Um, yes,' said Winsome, thinking fast. 'They *are* good costumes, aren't they? It's hard to believe they're made out of toilet-roll tubes.'

'Humph,' said Mrs Knowall, and she got out a black book and made a note.

Winsome steered Mrs Knowall away from the snake-like queue for the sea-serpent ride, but Mrs Knowall stopped dead three stalls on.

'Look at that!' she exclaimed.

The bouncy castle was busy with eager children bouncing up-and-up-and-up-and-up and dowwwwwwwwwwn. At the top of their jumps the children who weren't making faces at people in the tower block opposite were snatching sunbeams to eat on the way down.

'They've got that castle pumped up *far* too much,' snapped Mrs Knowall, writing something else in her black book.

'Oh, I don't think so,' said Winsome. 'It's all the... the exercise we get in school. You know, knee-bends and arm-stretches and things. It means we're all terribly fit and good at jumping.'

'Humph,' said Mrs Knowall. 'Well, what's that going on over there?'

'Oh, that's nothing very interesting,' said Winsome, hastily, but Mrs Knowall had already set off across the grass to the place where three wizards, a dwarf and what appeared to be a large cat were kicking off the worm-charming competition.

The first worms were appearing out of the soil just as Mrs Knowall arrived. One of the wizards soon had his worms doing the hokey-cokey (impressive, considering they weren't equipped with arms or legs to put in and out), and the cat had soon got *his* worms to crochet themselves into the form of a pink, and rather slimy, rat. The most popular charmer, however, was the dwarf, whose worms quickly made a wonderfully life-like portrait of the Queen entirely out of worm casts.

'Um... environment,' explained Winsome, randomly. 'We make all our own compost and everything.'

Mrs Knowall frowned so ferociously that the dwarf dug himself a hasty hole and jumped down it, and she made another note.

'I shall be reporting everything to my friend Mr Ogersby, the District Chief Inspector of Schools,' she announced, peering round so nastily that one of the wizards turned himself into a pot plant.

'Come and see the tombola,' said Winsome, hastily. 'There are lots of interesting... er... tins of prunes.'

It was lucky that Mrs Knowall, for all her peering and spying, wasn't really very observant. She didn't spot the fact that that every time Slacker's big sister Violet passed them munching yet another cake she was, strangely, a little thinner, and Mrs Knowall didn't notice that the ponies on the pony rides came in candy colours and had horns sticking out of their foreheads. Even so, there was no way even Mrs Knowall could fail to notice that everyone who got to the front of the queue for the Treasure Hunt vanished the moment they stuck their pin in the map, so Winsome led her round the back of the Blood Donation Tent (Mr Bloodworth's family seemed to be running that) to avoid it.

Unfortunately this meant they came face to face with a little old lady.

Who was dressed entirely in seaweed.

Chapter Eleven

'Well,' said the little old lady, looking Mrs Knowall up and down. 'You look as if you could do with some cheering up. Like to have your fortune told, would you? Only fifty pee for ten minutes!'

'What?' said Mrs Knowall. 'Pay money to a fraud? Certainly not.'

The old lady drew herself up tall. That brought her head up to the level of Winsome's shoulder.

'A *fraud*?' she echoed, outraged. 'I'll have you know the Mayor of Bognor always relies on Barry and me when he's working out his dates for the sardine dancing!'

A tall dark man in a cloak appeared at Mrs Knowall's elbow. He smiled charmingly, his fangs glistening in the afternoon sunshine.

'Perhaps you'd prefer a sit-down in the Blood Donation Tent,' he suggested, smoothly. 'We serve free tea. *Afterwards...*'

'Well, that sounds –' began Mrs Knowall, but before she could say any more, Winsome grabbed her arm and pushed her through the flap of Miss C Weed's tent into the cool stinky darkness.

'Mr Ogersby's bound to want to know all about the fortune-telling,' Winsome told her.

Mrs Knowall looked round, disapprovingly, but she sat down on a stool.

Miss C Weed tapped gently on the goldfish bowl with her knobbly knuckles.

'Barr-y!' she cooed. 'Here's someone who wants their fortune told!'

Barry opened his mouth wide in what might have been a yawn, and then, almost too quickly for the eye to follow, his head shot out of the bowl and picked up one of the cards that were scattered about the table.

Miss C Weed took the card reverently from Barry's mouth, turned it over, and read it out loud.

'*HAS SHE PAID?*' she read.

'I'll pay,' said Winsome, quickly, afraid that Mr Bloodsworth's relative might still be prowling about outside. 'But I've only got a pound.'

Miss C Weed took it happily.

'You can have *twenty* minutes fortune-telling for that,' she said. 'All right, Barry?'

Barry reared up out of his bowl and looked Mrs Knowall straight in the eye. Then he shuddered slightly and made three lightning strikes at three more cards, which he placed in Miss C Weed's scaly hands. Then he ducked back under the water and appeared to go back to sleep.

'There's a love,' said Miss C Weed, fondly. 'Right, so this is your fortune, ma'am, as told by Barry, the one and only *eel of fortune!*'

★ ★ ★

'A total fraud!' snapped Mrs Knowall, as she shouldered her way out of the tent and into the sunshine. 'I shall report her to the police!'

Winsome's heart sank. It was going to be bad enough having the District Chief Inspector investigating the school, without having the Fraud Squad joining in, too.

'I don't think it was a *fraud*, exactly,' she ventured.

'*Not a fraud?*' snapped Mrs Knowall. 'When the eel predicted that in a few minutes I'll see a member of the royal family turn into a frog?'

'Well,' said Winsome, helplessly, 'that *is* quite surprising, but –'

'– and that the mayor will win the wellie-wanging competition, even though I know for a fact that he's on holiday on some Pacific island?'

'Well –'

'And that there'll be white flakes falling within the hour? *Snow?* On the hottest day of the year? How can that be anything but a fraud?'

Winsome opened her mouth and then closed it again.

'I don't know,' she said, in a small voice.

Mrs Knowall snorted.

'I suppose there *is* a policeman on duty?' she asked.

'Um –'

'Hey, you!' Mrs Knowall shouted. 'Boy who looks like a bald gerbil!'

Jack looked as scared as if he'd come face to face with a vampire – which was odd, because actually coming face to face with a vampire earlier hadn't bothered him.

'Find me a policeman!' Mrs Knowall ordered. 'Quickly!'

Jack made a noise like a dying turnip and ran away as fast as he could. Winsome watched him go with envy as Mrs Knowall glared round at the happy crowds.

'Ah,' she said, with some satisfaction. 'There's my friend Mr Prince. He's a judge. He'll do!'

Mrs Knowall stormed across the field past the crocheted toilet-roll covers on the tombola stall and Winsome ran after her.

'What's up?' asked Anil. He was making a tour of the field to make sure the unicorns hadn't deposited anything anyone could trip over. 'Mrs Knowall hasn't noticed that the dinosaur slide is actually a dragon, has she?'

Winsome explained about the eel of fortune.

'But we can't have the school taken to court!' said Anil, in horror. 'We'll be fined – and we'll probably all end up in jail. Where's this Mr Prince?'

Mr Prince was at Slacker's cake stall.

'Delicious!' he said, through some crumbs. 'Marvellous! Wonderful! Six more, please.'

Slacker shook his head regretfully.

'I think you've had enough, Mr Prince,' he said.

'No, no, it's all right,' said Mr Prince. 'I'm wearing an elasticated belt. And these cakes are *so* delicious!'

'Yes,' said Slacker, patiently. 'But as well as all those Lean Tarts you've had four of the

More-on-Top Cakes, haven't you. Any more and you'll be getting side-effects.'

Slacker turned to serve another customer just as Mrs Knowall arrived at Mr Prince's side.

'Mr Prince!' she snapped. 'I wish to report a fraud!'

'Really?' said Mr Prince, absently, taking the opportunity while Slacker's back was turned to help himself to three more Lean Tarts. 'Mmm! Superb! Have you tried one of these, Mrs Knowall?'

'No I haven't,' she said. 'And what's more I –' she broke off and looked at Mr Prince closely. 'Are you all right?' she asked. 'Because you're looking a little... green.'

'He does, too,' said Serise, wandering up. '*And* his eyes have gone all high-up and bulgy.'

Mr Prince suddenly let out a resounding burp. He clapped his hand to his mouth in embarrassment – and that was when they saw that his fingers were even greener than his face. They were webbed, too. And not only that, but –

'He's *shrinking*,' gasped Anil. And he was: he was soon as short as Anil, and then as short as the table, and then...

'Eek!' screamed Mrs Knowall, jumping backwards, because instead of a full-sized judge all that was left was a heap of clothes with something jumping about inside it.

Slacker looked round.

'Oh, is that another one?' he asked. 'Honestly, people *won't* be told, will they? Here, write PRINCE on this label, will you? I'm bundling their clothes up and putting them under the table for safekeeping.'

A small green nose wearing Mr Prince's glasses appeared from under a vest.

'And what about the... er... frog?' asked Anil, once the clothes were bundled and labelled.

'Oh, he'll be back to normal in a couple of hours,' said Slacker. 'Just put him in the washing-up bowl with the others.'

Mrs Knowall was looking nearly as green as Mr Prince.

'Hey, it's a good job you didn't say anything to Mr Prince about the eel of fortune being a fraud, isn't it, Mrs Knowall,' Anil told her, cheerfully. 'He'd probably have put you in prison for slander.'

'But – but – but – that was only one prediction!' blustered Mrs Knowall, a bit cross-eyed. 'That could have been a simple coinci –'

There was a great cry of *watch out!* and everyone ducked as a boot flew over their heads.

'Look at that,' said Anil. 'Rodney's wanged the wellie *miles*.'

Serise, running up to find the wellie, shrugged.

'He still won't beat the mayor,' she said. 'The mayor wanged his wellie nearly as far as the Trifle Range.'

Mrs Knowall jumped as if someone had plugged her into a socket.

'The mayor?' she yelped. 'But he's away on holiday in the middle of the Pacific Ocean!'

There was an awkward pause as a pair of goblins with tape measures ran out, measured the length of Rodney's throw, and then signalled a thumbs-down.

'I told you the mayor would win,' said Serise, as the centaur running the wellie-wanging presented a silver cup to a very tanned man wearing a knotted handkerchief and a glittering chain of office. 'Trust him to go on holiday to the island where the Treasure Hunt is taking place. Though I don't think those pirates should have let him travel on a Treasure Hunt ticket, myself.'

Mrs Knowall was very pale. She kept looking up at the sky as if expecting to be carried off by a giant eagle.

'Good, Barry the eel of fortune, isn't he,' said Anil, pointedly. 'A bargain, too, at a pound for twenty minutes.'

'Especially when it was my pound,' said Winsome, sighing.

Mrs Knowall was definitely looking cross-eyed, now.

'You'd better take her somewhere quiet,' advised Anil. 'I don't think she can stand much more excitement. It's a pity the trolls have eaten all the tins of prunes on the tombola, or you could have taken her there.'

'I'll take her round behind the helter-skelter,' suggested Winsome. 'There's not much going on there now the jelly-dancers have finished.'

'Everything's nearly finished,' said Jack, sadly, wandering up. He was wearing a paper bag over his head. Presumably it made him feel safer with Mrs Knowall around. 'The last sea-serpent trip has set off,' he went on, 'and the last Thirty-Eight-Point-Eight-Nine-Two Kilometre Boot Tour has gone as well. Oh, and look, there's Emily taking the unicorns their home-time buckets of fairy cakes. Still, it's been brilliant, hasn't it? We've made tons and *tons* of money.'

Winsome and Jack led Mrs Knowall to a bench. A group of fairies was occupying it, but they disappeared hastily – instantly – when they saw Mrs Knowall. To be fair, though, they may have been disturbed by the approach of a huge and extremely grubby troll, who was coming along carrying the biggest dustbin any of them had ever seen, filled to the brim with rubbish for his supper.

The troll gradually realised he'd entered a dead end, and slowly wondered what to do (trolls are notoriously slow thinkers). He looked around, puzzled, scratching his head... and then suddenly Mrs Knowall let out a squawk like a hen laying a square egg.

Because it was *snowing*. Large white flakes were drifting down lazily from the clear blue summer sky, swooping and dipping to lay themselves delicately on the ground.

Jack raised his paper bag a few inches so he could see better.

'But it's really hot,' he said, in bewilderment, 'and there's not a cloud in the sky. How can it be snowing?'

'I don't know,' said Winsome, just as puzzled.

'Hey, and that's not the only funny thing,' said Jack. 'What's that noise that sounds like someone rubbing a hedgehog against a fence?'

They all looked up and down, and left and right, and discovered that it was only snowing just by the bench: the rest of the field was quivering with heat.

Serise came trotting round the corner and stopped short when she saw the circle of snow.

'Ew!' she said. 'That's just *disgusting*!'

'Disgusting?' said Winsome.

'Yes,' said Serise. '*Completely* disgusting. You're not going to tell me you *like* standing there with that troll scratching his horrible bristly head and covering you in his revolting dandruff!'

Winsome and Jack squawked and ran hastily out of the dandruff shower – but Mrs Knowall only swayed a bit, blinking, as the snowy flakes pirouetted round her. First she went nearly as white as the dandruff itself (it was amazing how such white dandruff had come off such a grubby head), and then she went pink, and then she went red. And then – though this was surely impossible – Serise, Jack and Winsome all agreed afterwards that her ears started *steaming*.

'Are you all right, Mrs Knowall?' asked Winsome.

Mrs Knowall's eyes began bulging as if there was some great pressure building up inside her.

As the children began to back cautiously away, Slacker and Emily and Anil spotted them from across the field and rushed up to join them, flushed with the success of the afternoon.

They arrived just in time to see Mrs Knowall go completely *bananas*.

Chapter Twelve

Mrs Knowall took in a huge breath that swelled her horrible snot-coloured dress to bursting point and then she let out a roar like a rampaging rhinoceros: '**Magic!!!**' she bellowed.

'Hmm,' Anil said. 'Perhaps it wasn't such a good thing that the eel of fortune's predictions came true, after all.'

'Now she'll report us to Mr Ogersby,' said Jack, from inside his paper bag. 'And he'll sack the teachers, and then the place will turn into an ordinary school!'

'What can we *do*?' asked Emily, in despair.

'Blackmail?' suggested Serise. 'Feed her lots of cakes, and then threaten to post a photo on the Internet of her turning into a frog?'

'We can't do that!' said Winsome.

'No,' said Slacker. 'There aren't any cakes left.'

'Do you think the fairies could magic her away?' whispered Emily.

'Fairies? You'd need a troll to move Mrs Knowall,' said Serise.

'Well, a troll, then,' suggested Anil.

'No,' said Winsome, firmly. 'We couldn't possibly.'

'Why not?' asked Jack.

'Because Winsome's a goody-goody,' said Serise.

'Because even trolls have standards,' said Winsome.

The echoes of Mrs Knowall's roar had died away and she was taking in another long breath. The children braced themselves.

'**You just wait until my friend Mr Ogersby the District Chief Inspector of Schools gets to hear about this!**' Mrs Knowall bellowed. '**Eels of fortune! Poisonous cakes –**'

'They weren't *poisonous* –' objected Slacker, but his words were swept away in a tide of fury.

'**Mayors thousands of miles away from where they should be! Judges turning into frogs! Dandruff-infested giants –**'

'That was a troll, actually,' Anil pointed out, and then said *ouch!* when Serise gave him a dig in the ribs.

But it was too late, Mrs Knowall had heard him.

'**A troll?**' she shouted, shaking her fist in the air. '*A troll?* **What business has a *troll* got at a respectable school?**'

'They're really good at eating the rubbish,' said Jack, helpfully. 'Even non-recyclable stuff like polystyrene and dragon scales and greasy paper bags.'

'They don't even mind if the bags have got wasps in them,' Slacker added. 'They just munch everything up, ring-pulls and all. It's really eco-friendly.'

Mrs Knowall turned her eyes incredulously to the sky – and then she began doing her nut again.

'**What are all those things flying about?**' she shrieked.

Class Six looked. Most of the things flying about were gnats, but there were also several fairies and one or two ladies on broomsticks who were best not even thought about.

'What things?' asked Jack, innocently, pulling his paper bag back down firmly over his eyes.

'**Those things with tall pointy hats!**' howled Mrs Knowall, as Rodney strolled up happily.

'**And those things sprinkling glitter all over the place from their wands!**'

'Oh, don't worry about the glitter,' said Emily, with surprising bravery. 'The unicorns will clear that up.'

'*Unicorns????*'

Rodney gave one of his slow patient smiles.

'There's no such thing as unicorns,' he told Mrs Knowall, kindly. 'Those are just popsicle solutions.'

But Mrs Knowall wasn't listening. Now that her mind had been opened she was suddenly seeing magic everywhere. Those short men with the beards walking along singing *hi-ho hi-ho...* that group of tall dark people with red-tipped fangs... and that man over there with the fluff of fur sticking out of the bottom of his trouser leg...

Her next words were more of a scream than a bellow: '**Mr Wolfe is a werewolf!**' she screamed, and then, as Serise was muttering something about the clue being in the name, unfortunately the dinosaur-slide dragon walked past on his way home with his ladder over his shoulder.

Mrs Knowall gasped twice, and then once more – and then her bones all suddenly seemed to turn to rubber, and she folded down on to the ground in a dead faint.

Class Six waited until they were sure she wasn't going to leap up again and start biting them, and then they stepped cautiously closer. Winsome, who was ridiculously sensible and kind, took hold of Mrs Knowall's wrist.

'She's still alive,' she said.

Serise sighed.

'Ah well,' she said. 'I suppose you can't have everything.'

'We'd better tell a grown-up,' said Emily.

The others looked at each other.

'I suppose we should,' said Anil, reluctantly, and went over to where Mr Bloodsworth and Miss Elwig were supervising the taking down of the marquee. There was someone else with them, a stout, red-haired man in a checked suit. Even though it was the hottest afternoon of the year, he had a scarf wrapped round his face and he was wearing brown leather gloves.

That was quite odd – but then *quite odd* was hardly noticeable among the crowds of people making their happy way home bearing gold doubloons, or jam jars containing baby octopuses.

'Please, Mr Bloodsworth,' said Anil. 'Mrs Knowall's fainted.'

The red-haired man looked round. 'Mrs Knowall?' he said, his voice rather muffled and growly. 'Do you mean Mrs *Pomposa* Knowall?'

Miss Elwig sighed.

'That's her,' she said.

The red-haired man frowned.

'I've had an absolute *pile* of letters from Pomposa recently,' he said.

Mrs Elwig gulped.

'Um... what did they say?' she asked, running her hand nervously through her hair and disturbing a small cod and several chips.

'Oh, I haven't opened them,' said the red-haired man. 'They'll be complaints. That's all Pomposa ever does, complain. Dreadful woman! What on earth is she doing at your school fair?'

Mr Bloodsworth murmured something about her wanting to become Chairman of the School Governors.

'But the woman's a complete menace!' said the red-haired man, appalled. 'Why, she *hates* children!'

'Grown-ups, too,' said Miss Elwig, sadly.

'Well, you must make sure she doesn't get the job,' said the red-haired man.

'But we can't,' said Anil, earnestly. 'Mrs Knowall is friends with Mr Ogersby, the District Chief Inspector of Schools, so she's *bound* to get the job. And when she does, she'll change everything!'

'But why on earth would she want to do that?' the red-haired man asked. 'I've never seen so many people at a school fair. Or such happy, clever children. Why, the boy running the cake stall seemed to know all his times tables up to *at least* his nine hundred and ninety-nines.'

'She wants us to be ordinary,' said Anil, sadly. 'Ordinary and boring and just like everybody else.'

The red-haired man snorted.

'You mean Mrs Knowall wants to make this a place where all the children are squeezed into the same shape, so the fat ones can't breathe and the thin ones rattle?'

Anil nodded sadly.

The red-haired man seemed to swell a little.

'Well, we'll soon see about *that*,' he said.

He marched over to where Mrs Knowall lay on the ground surrounded by the rest of Class Six.

'Let me through!' he ordered. 'I've come to take her away!'

Class Six looked at each other.

Serise stepped aside with a be-my-guest gesture, but the others didn't budge. The red-haired man looked from one to the other of them in amazement.

'Don't you *want* her taken away?' he asked.

'That would be very kind,' admitted Winsome. 'But...'

'It would make Mrs Knowall cross,' said Emily, sadly.

'She'd go and tell Mr Ogersby,' said Jack.

'And that would be the end of everything,' said Slacker, gloomily.

The red-haired man gave a jolly laugh and pulled off his gloves to reveal hands covered in fur. Then he pulled his scarf from his face to show a great thrusting jaw and some sharp fangs.

Emily clapped a hand to her mouth.

'An ogre!' she squeaked.

The red-haired man smiled at her indulgently.

'An ogre?' he echoed. 'No, my dear child, I'm not *an* ogre. I'm *the* ogre!'

He strode forward, picked up Mrs Knowall, and slung her over a mighty shoulder.

'I,' he went on, triumphantly, 'am Mr Obadiah Ogersby. Have you heard of me? The District Chief Inspector of Schools?'

The children gasped.

'And do you know what that means?' he demanded.

'Not exactly,' admitted Slacker.

The ogre gave a very wide grin indeed.

'It means that what I say, goes. And do you know something? Mrs Pomposa Knowall is most *definitely* going to go!'

And, giving Class Six a cheery wave and a large wink, he carried her away.

★　★　★

Mrs Broom was back at school on Monday morning.

'How was training college, Miss Broom?' asked Emily, after Miss Broom had given Algernon the snake a hug and Class Six had told her all about the school fair.

'Not too bad,' said Miss Broom. 'Rather dull, of course, but it made a change. I'm glad I didn't have to go this week: they've got a new head starting. Someone with a silly name. Pomposa, I think.'

Class Six stared at her in wonder.

'Pomposa?' asked Serise. 'As in Pomposa Knowall?'

Miss Broom smiled her wide warm smile.

'The very same,' she said. 'She'll be very happy there, I should imagine, lecturing teachers on rules and regulations.'

'But who will be the new Chairman of the School Governors?' said Emily.

Miss Broom laughed, a wild witchy laugh full of midnight and magic and all the most shiveringly exciting things in the whole world.

'We thought we'd ask someone who's an expert on being green,' she said.

'What, a frog?' asked Jack, a little surprised.

'No, no,' said Miss Broom. 'A recycling expert.'

Anil's hand shot up.

'I know,' he said. 'A troll! They can turn *anything* into manure.'

'And while they have enormous appetites for slime and grime, they have no appetite *at all* for interfering,' said Miss Broom.

'Brilliant!' said Jack – but Rodney frowned.

'Trolls don't exist,' he said.

Class Six looked at him disbelievingly.

'But you saw them!' said Slacker. 'Those massive potato-headed things licking out the dustbins!'

'They even ate all those old tins of prunes from the tombola,' said Winsome.

Rodney smiled and shook his head.

'Those weren't trolls,' he said.

Anil clutched his hair.

'You think a human being would eat twenty tins of prunes?' he demanded. '*Without opening them?*'

'Of course they would,' said Rodney. He laughed. 'Honestly, your memories! You've been saying for days that's why everything happens: because of *the meal of more prunes*!'

Class Six groaned.

'We're doomed, aren't we,' said Anil, hopelessly. 'However much the wheel of fortune turns, we'll always have Rodney.'

Miss Broom smiled.

'We'll always have Rodney and *magic*,' she said. 'Lovely, sparkling, mysterious and marvellous magic. I think that's worth three cheers, don't you?'

'Hurray!' Class Six shouted, because it was. '*Hurray!* Hurray for mer-mer-mer-mer-*maggots*!'

'What maggots?' asked Rodney.

Bonus Bits!

GUESS WHO?

Match the pieces of information below to the people in the story. Check your answers at the end of this section (no peeking!).

1 Winsome
2 Slacker Punchkin
3 Miss Broom
4 Anil
5 Emily
6 Jack
7 Mrs Knowall
8 Rodney
9 Serise

A always a couple of conversations behind the others
B always keen to get down to business
C never has much patience with anyone
D studious, responsible and hard-working
E has ears like satellite dishes and a nose like a vacuum cleaner
F does exciting magic for her class
G always hungry and often eating
H always worried about everything
I known for doing silly things

QUIZ TIME!

Can you remember what happens in the story? Flick back in the book if you need help. There are answers at the end (but no peeking before you finish!).

1. Who was being strangled by the beanstalk?
A Slacker Punchkin
B Miss Elwig
C Emily
D Winsome

2. Who made a Mrs Knowall alarm system?
A Miss Broom
B Miss Elwig
C Miss Jeanie
D Anil

3. Which teacher loves spending time underwater?
A Miss Broom
B Miss Elwig
C Mr Wolfe
D Mr Bloodsworth

4. What do you need to turn yourself into a porcupine?
A a magic wand

B pickled brains
C bat droppings
D dragon claw clippings

5. Who is in charge of all the teachers in the area?
A Mr Werewolf
B Mr Ogresbreath
C Mr Bloodsworth
D Mr Ogersby

6. What is the name of Class Six's pet?
A Algebra
B Algernon
C Algerithem
D Algerian

7. Who run the firework rides at the school fair?
A The green men
B The Brownies
C The flying ladies
D The students

8. Who is the supply teacher for Class Six?
A Mr Chestnut
B Mr Yew
C Mr Hazel
D Mr Oak

WHAT NEXT?

- If you enjoyed reading this story, why not look for other school stories or magic stories to read?
- Class Six have had lots of exciting adventures with Miss Broom like flying in the hall and going down a meerkat burrow. If you were in Class Six what magic would you ask Miss Broom to do? Why not write a story describing your adventure with Class Six and Miss Broom.

ANSWERS to GUESS WHO
1D, 2G, 3F, 4B, 5H, 6I, 7E, 8A, 9C

ANSWERS to QUIZ TIME
1A, 2C, 3B, 4D, 5D, 6B, 7A, 8C

If you enjoyed this story why not look out for Class Six's first adventure...

Turn over for a sneak peak!

Class Six and the Nits of Doom

Chapter One

It was the first day back at school after the summer holidays and the playground was full of excited children. Class Three were hopping up and down inside their enormous new school coats, and Classes Four and Five were charging about shouting WE WENT TO THE SEASIDE AND EVERYWHERE SMELLED OF EGGIES! or else huddled in groups comparing hair clips.

But just inside the school gate there was another group of children. They were a bit bigger than the others, but they weren't excited or running about. These children had pale faces, and eyes that glittered with fear. From time to time a trembling child crept in through the school gate to join them, but not one of them took a single step nearer the school than was absolutely necessary.

One boy was just looking at his watch, as if in some forlorn hope that the hands would start going backwards, when from a long way off there came a rattling. It came closer and closer until a small car came into view. Its bumper was tied on with string, its wings were patched with duct tape, and it was covered in grime and rust.

'Here comes Rodney,' said the boy with the watch.

The car stopped by the school gate and one of the doors flapped open. Out of the opening came a large foot. And then another.

All the children, their faces blue with terror, stared at the boy who got out of the car.

Rodney waved a big hand at them.

'I span round really fast fifty-three times last night,' he said, proudly. 'And I *still* wasn't sick!'

And then he shouldered his way through the group of children by the gate and strolled happily down towards the school building.

There was a long pause as the children watched Rodney walk away.

'He's not scared,' said Jack, at last.

'Of course he's not,' said Serise grumpily. 'He's too stupid to be scared. I bet Rodney's too stupid to be scared of a charging bull, even. Or a runaway double-decker bus. Or a shark jumping out of the canal with its jaws wide open.'

'Or a witch,' said Emily, in a small voice. Everyone froze. Then they all nodded sadly.

'The bell will be going soon.' Anil looked at his watch again. 'And then we'll *have* to go in, won't we.'

Emily started crying.

'Four minutes, exactly,' went on Anil. 'Three minutes fifty-five seconds. Three minutes fifty—' Slacker Punchkin put a flabby arm absent-mindedly round Anil's neck and tried to strangle him.

'The trouble with Rodney is that he doesn't believe there's any such thing as witches,' Slacker said. 'He's just like a grown-up that way.'

'Yes,' said Serise scornfully. 'Stupid.'

'I mean, even my dad said it was silly to worry about a witch,' went on Slacker.

Winsome rescued Anil. 'Perhaps it *is* silly.'

Emily sniffed sadly. 'But we've all seen it,' she said.

'Magic, all over the whole school. And we saw how peculiar last year's Year Six went.'

'I suppose so,' agreed Winsome, frowning. 'But then we never heard any of them actually say *my class teacher Miss Broom is a witch*, did we?'

'That's true,' said Jack, perking up a bit.

Serise turned on him with contempt. 'No,' she snapped. 'But I've heard them say *Miss Broom's a winter vest!* and *Miss Broom's a weasel's nostril!*'

Emily started crying again.

'Yes,' agreed Anil. 'Just as if something was stopping them saying the word *witch*. Just as if they were all under some spell which stopped them telling anyone about it.'

Winsome tried to look brave. 'Well, at least year's Year Six all survived, didn't they? I mean, they didn't end up turned into toadstools or piglets or anything.'

There was a short pause.

'Although we never did find out where all those rhinoceroses came from that were out in the playing field that day,' Anil pointed out.

Jack suddenly grinned.

'Hey, it'd be brilliant to be a rhino,' he said. 'If I was a rhino I'd charge right through the Co-op spearing doughnuts on my horn and no one would be able to stop me.'

'Oh yes they would,' snapped Serise. 'Someone would shoot you.'

Anil looked at his watch again. 'It's nearly time for the bell,' he said. 'Ten... nine...'

'No they wouldn't!' said Jack. 'Rhinos have armour-plated skin, don't they? And anyway they're really rare so you're not allowed to shoot them, not even if they charge right into car parks and start crushing all the cars with their enormous great feet, and—'

'... two... one...'

BRRRRRRRRRRRRRRRRRRRR RRRRRRRRRRRIIIIIIIIIIIIIIIIIIIIIIIII NNNNNNNNNNNNNNNNGGGGGGGGGG GGGGGGGGGGGGGG!!!!!!!!!!!!!!

All the children jumped several centimetres into the air and clutched at each other in terror, and several of them screamed.

Slacker Punchkin shook his head sadly.

'That's it,' he said. 'There's no escape, now. We're doomed.'

Emily began jumping up and down.

'I don't want to die I don't want to die I don't want to die!' she shrieked, but Winsome put her arm round her.

'You'll be all right,' Winsome said. 'Miss Broom would be sent to prison if she did anything bad to us. You know that really. Come on.'

The rest of Class Six looked at each other, and the sound of their knocking knees could be heard even above the chattering of all the other classes as they filed into school.

And then Class Six sighed, and they slowly and reluctantly began to trudge down the school path towards their new classroom.

And towards their new teacher, Miss Broom.

The witch.